This
PJ BOOK
belongs to

PJ Library®

JEWISH BEDTIME STORIES and SONGS

When Joseph is a baby, his grandfather makes him a wonderful blanket. But as Joseph grows older, the blanket becomes tattered and worn. *Throw it out!* cries Joseph's mother.

Luckily, grandpa is an extraordinary tailor. He can fix anything! And so with a snip! snip! here, and a few stitches there, Grandpa transforms the treasured blanket into a jacket, a vest, a Sabbath tie, a handkerchief, and finally a beautiful button.

But when the button is lost, even Grandpa can't help. After all, how can you make something from nothing?

In a rich and loving portrait of *shtetl* life, Phoebe Gilman presents a traditional Jewish folktale about family love and ingenuity that will warm the hearts of readers young and old.

Phoebe Gilman grew up in the Bronx, New York, and studied art in the United States, Israel, and Europe. Before beginning her career as a writer and illustrator of children's books, she taught art for fifteen years. She created six previous books for young readers, including *The Wonderful Pigs of Jillian Jiggs* and *Grandma and the Pirates*.

PHOEBE GILMAN

Something from Nothing

Adapted from a Jewish folktale

SCHOLASTIC INC.
New York

For Irving Hirschorn
Our Uncle
We remember you with love.

Published by Scholastic Inc., 557 Broadway, New York, NY, 10012 by arrangement with North Winds Press.
SCHOLASTIC and associated logos are trademarks and/or registered trademarks of Scholastic Inc.

Library of Congress Cataloging-in-Publication Data

Gilman, Phoebe, 1940–2002
   Something from nothing: adapted from a Jewish folktale / Phoebe Gilman.
     p.   cm.
   Summary: In this retelling of a traditional Jewish folktake, Joseph's baby blanket is transformed into ever smaller
items as he grows until there is nothing left—but then Joseph has an idea.
    ISBN 0-590-47280-1 [1. Folklore, Jewish.] I. Title.   PZ8.1.G445So   1993   398.21—dc20
[E]   92-37587
                                           CIP
                                         AC

ISBN: 978-1-338-32840-0
10 9 8 7 6 5 4 3 2   22 23 24 25 26
Printed in the U.S.A.   76
This book was originally published in hardcover by Scholastic Hardcover in 1992.
This edition first printing 2018

Artist's note:
The paintings for this book were done in oil and egg tempera on gessoed D'Arches satin finish watercolor paper.
Beginning with a colored imprimatur (a thin layer of reddish ochre paint wiped on with a rag) the paintings were built up
in alternating layers of egg tempera and oil glazes.

1022/B1280/A3

When Joseph was a baby, his grandfather made him a wonderful blanket . . .

1

. . . to keep him warm and cozy and to chase away bad dreams.

But as Joseph grew older, the wonderful blanket grew older too.

One day his mother said to him, "Joseph, look at your blanket. It's frazzled, it's worn, it's unsightly, it's torn. It is time to throw it out."

"Grandpa can fix it," Joseph said.
Joseph's grandfather took the blanket and turned it round and round.

"Hmm," he said as his scissors went snip, snip, snip and his needle flew in and out and in and out, "There's just enough material here to make . . ."

. . . a wonderful jacket. Joseph put on the wonderful jacket and went outside to play.

But as Joseph grew older, the wonderful jacket grew older too.

One day his mother said to him, "Joseph, look at your jacket. It's shrunken and small, doesn't fit you at all. It is time to throw it out!"

"Grandpa can fix it," Joseph said.
Joseph's grandfather took the jacket and turned it
round and round.

"Hmm," he said as his scissors went snip, snip, snip and his needle flew in and out and in and out, "There's just enough material here to make . . ."

9

. . . a wonderful vest. Joseph wore the wonderful vest to school the very next day.

But as Joseph grew older, the wonderful vest grew older too.

One day his mother said to him, "Joseph, look at your vest! It's spotted with glue and there's paint on it too. It is time to throw it out!"

"Grandpa can fix it," Joseph said.
Joseph's grandfather took the vest and turned it
round and round.

"Hmm," he said as his scissors went snip, snip, snip
and his needle flew in and out and in and out,
"There's just enough material here to make . . ."

. . . a wonderful tie. Joseph wore the wonderful tie to his grandparents' house every Friday.

But as Joseph grew older, his wonderful tie grew older too.

One day his mother said to him, "Joseph, look at your tie! This big stain of soup makes the end of it droop. It is time to throw it out!"

"Grandpa can fix it," Joseph said.
Joseph's grandfather took the tie and turned it round and round.

"Hmm," he said as his scissors went snip, snip, snip and his needle flew in and out and in and out, "There's just enough material here to make . . ."

17

. . . a wonderful handkerchief. Joseph used the wonderful handkerchief to keep his pebble collection safe.

But as Joseph grew older, his wonderful handkerchief grew older too.

One day his mother said to him, "Joseph, look at your handkerchief! It's been used till it's tattered, it's splotched and it's splattered. It is time to THROW IT OUT!"

"Grandpa can fix it," Joseph said.
Joseph's grandfather took the handkerchief and
turned it round and round.

"Hmm," he said as his scissors went snip, snip, snip and his needle flew in and out and in and out, "There's just enough material here to make . . ."

21

. . . a wonderful button. Joseph wore the wonderful button on his suspenders to hold his pants up.

One day his mother said to him, "Joseph, where is your button?"
Joseph looked. It was gone!

He searched everywhere but he could not find it.
Joseph ran down to his grandfather's house.

24

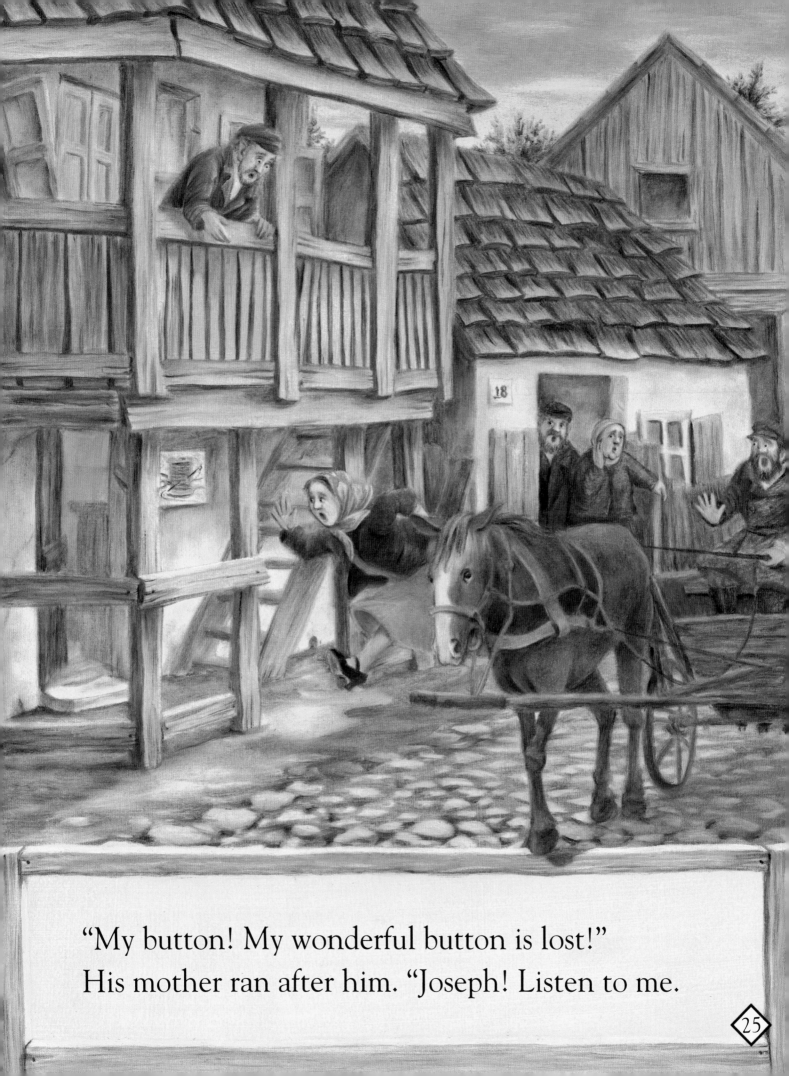

"My button! My wonderful button is lost!"
His mother ran after him. "Joseph! Listen to me.

"The button is gone, finished, kaput. Even your grandfather can't make something from nothing." Joseph's grandfather shook his head sadly. "I'm afraid that your mother is right," he said.

The next day Joseph went to school. "Hmm," he said, as his pen went scritch scratch, scritch scratch, over the paper. "There's just enough material here to make . . ."

. . . a wonderful story.